Molly
AND THE
Magic
Wishbone

BARBARA MCCLINTOCK

FRANCES FOSTER BOOKS · FARRAR, STRAUS AND GIROUX · NEW YORK

To Larson, Valerie, Georgia, and Charlotte,
with love and thanks for
being the inspiration for Molly and her family

Mama was in bed with a very bad cold, so Molly put on her cloak and hat and set out to buy a fish for dinner.

"Excuse me," said an old woman. "I will tell you a secret. You will find a bone in your portion of fish tonight. Save it, because it will be a magic wishbone, worth one wish for anything you want in the whole world. I know, because I'm your Fairy Godmother. But use your wish wisely. You get only one." And she vanished—poof! Gone.

Am I dreaming? thought Molly. She shook her head and went home.

But, sure enough, that night, right after all the fish was eaten, one thin white bone was left on Molly's plate.

It must be true!

Phylis and Alice and Timmy and John gathered around and looked at the bone.

It must be true!

Molly wiped off the bone and put it in her pocket and went upstairs to her room.

Phylis and Alice and Timmy and John all wanted to know what she'd wish for—especially Phylis, who was the youngest.

"A room full of toys?"
"A dress just like Penelope Porterhouse Pitts's?"
"A horse?"
"A big house full of palm trees and slithery snakes?"
"A lifetime supply of cakes and candies?"

To each of these things Molly said no, no, no, no, and no. Nothing sounded quite right to use the wishbone for.

"I'll just wait until I know exactly what I really want," she said.

"Molly! Molly! Come quick! Our rabbit is very sick!"
"Are you going to use the wishbone to make her well?"

"No," said Molly. "But fetch me a box and a warm blanket and a bowl of water."

Molly stayed with the rabbit until—
"Come in!"—there were six baby rabbits!

"Molly! Molly! Come quick!
Timmy broke Mama's best bowl!"

"Surely *now* you can use your wish to put it back the way it was!"

But Molly set right to work and got a pot of glue and put all the
bitty little pieces back together again. And the bowl was good as new.

"Molly! Molly! This time it's really bad!"
"Use your wishbone now! There's a really horrible ghost in our room!"
"We're so scared we can't sleep!"
"Oh, phoo!" said Molly, lighting a candle. "It's nothing but a shirt hanging on a chair."

Molly calmed the little ones and read them a story and tucked them into bed, and they all fell asleep right away.

By the next morning, the little ones had forgotten about the wishbone—except for Phylis, who was the youngest.

Molly was saving her wish for something special—but what? If *she* had a magic wishbone, she'd have no trouble thinking of a wish.

Maybe, thought Phylis, I can get my own wishbone!

She put on her hat and cloak and slipped out the door.

She had an idea of where the fish market was—she took a left, a right, two lefts, and another right—and was, without a doubt, completely lost!

When Molly woke up, she finally decided on a wish.

A closet full of beautiful silk dresses, she thought, with bows and lace, and matching hats, and shoes, and handbags, and velvet coats. And an umbrella, of course, in case of rain.

She held up the magic wishbone, closed her eyes, and began to wish.

"Molly! Molly! We need you!
Phylis is missing!"

Molly, more than a little annoyed at having her wish interrupted,
put on her hat and cloak and went out to look for Phylis.

She looked everywhere—but no Phylis! She walked until her feet hurt—no Phylis! She asked in shops, went down strange streets—no Phylis!

It was cold, the whole day almost done—and still no Phylis!

Molly finally returned home. It was dark, and she was so worried and frightened for Phylis that she felt sick.

Molly went directly to her room and took out the magic wishbone.

"I wish for Phylis to be home, safe and sound," she whispered, and wished with all her heart.

The wind rushed and snow circled around thickly. There was a knock at the door—it was the Fairy Godmother.

"Here," she said, "is Phylis."

Her arms opened—under her cape, cold but safe, stood Phylis.

Phylis was hugged and dried and wrapped in a blanket and put in a chair by the fire.

"All the things in the world would mean nothing without you," said Molly.

She made Phylis a cup of tea, and one for the Fairy Godmother, too.

The Fairy Godmother drank her tea, found little presents for everyone in the vast pockets of her cape, kissed them all on their heads, and went away—poof! Gone.

In the morning, Mama was feeling better, and heard all about the
magic wishbone for the rest of the day and for many days after.

Distributed in Canada by Douglas & McIntyre Ltd.

Color separations by Hong Kong Scanner Arts

Printed and bound in the United States of America by

Berryville Graphics

Designed by Filomena Tuosto

First edition, 2001

1 3 5 7 9 10 8 6 4 2

Library of Congress Cataloging-in-Publication Data

McClintock, Barbara.

Molly and the magic wishbone / Barbara McClintock. — 1st ed.

p.   cm.

"Frances Foster books."

Summary: Molly's fairy godmother gives her a magic fishbone that will grant one wish,
which the resourceful girl saves until she really needs it.

ISBN 0-374-34999-1

[1. Wishes—Fiction. 2. Brothers and sisters—Fiction.] I. Title.

PZ7.M47841418Mo 2001

[E]—dc21   98-31789